前　　言

　　語言的學習，愈早愈好。孩子的模仿力強、吸收能力佳，小孩子的發音在還沒有形成地方口音之前，就讓他學習說英語，可避免晚一天學，多一天困難的煩惱！外國語言的學習與刺激，有助於智力的開發，及見聞的增長。前教育部次長阮大年說：「早學英語的好處很多。我小學四年級就開始學英語，以致到了台灣唸中學，我一直名列前茅。」

　　英語是「容易學習，很難學好」的語言。雖然容易學習，方法不得要領，也等於徒勞。「學習兒童美語讀本」設計活潑而有趣的學習方式，讓兒童快快樂樂地學會說英語。

◆ 對小朋友而言：學習身邊的英語，能使兒童在開始學習英語時，有最直接而深刻的體驗。本套書以日常生活經常遇到的狀況為中心，提供一切能引起兒童興趣的學習題材。實用、生動而有創意的教材，讓孩子能自然親近趣味盎然的英語！

♥ 對教學者而言：本套書編序完整、內容循序漸進，教學者易於整理，各頁教材之下，均有教學提示，可供老師參考，不必多花時間，就可獲得事半功倍的準備效果。本套書也針對兒童學習心理，每單元均有唱歌、遊戲，或美勞，使教學者能在輕鬆愉快的方式下，順利教學！

♠ 對父母親而言：本套書的各單元均以日常生活為背景，也適合讓父母親來親自教導。在兒童心理學上，「親子教學法」對孩子學習能力的增強，有很大的幫助。本套書在每單元之後，均附有在家學習的方法，提供具體的方法和技巧，可以幫助家長與子女的共同學習！

　　透過這套書，兒童學習英語的過程，必然是輕鬆而愉快。而且，由於開始時所引發的興趣，未來的學習將會充滿興奮與期待！

本書的特色

· 學習語言的基本順序，是由 Hearing（聽）、Speaking（說）、Reading
（讀）、Writing（寫），本套教材即依此原則編輯。

· 內容背景本土化、國情化，使兒童在熟悉的環境中學習英語，以避免像其
他的原文兒童英語書，與現實生活有出入的弊端。

· 題材趣味化、生活化，學了立即能在日常生活中使用。

· 將英語歌曲、遊戲，具有創意的美勞，與學習英語巧妙地組合在一起，以
提高兒童的學習興趣，達到寓教於樂的目的。

· 每單元教材的形式一致，有效學習，方便教學。在書末並附有詳細的本書
學習內容一覽表，查閱方便。

· 每單元的教材均有教學指導和提示，容易教學。而且每單元之末均列有目
標說明，指導者易於掌握重點。

· 提供在家學習的方法，家長們可親自教導自己的子女學習英語，除加強親
子關係外，也達到自然的學習成效。

· 每單元終了，附有考查學習成果的習作，有助於指導者了解學生的吸收力。

· 書末附有單元總複習，並收錄所有的生字圖，以加深學習印象。另外，在
下一冊書的前面部分也有各種方式的複習，以達到溫故知新的目的。

· 本套書是以六歲兒童到國一學生為對象，內容自成一系統，可供不同程度
的學習。

CONTENTS

1. GREETINGS

Good morning.

Good afternoon.

Good evening.

Good night.

Note: First of all, you can draw some clocks on the board and say "Good morning-Good afternoon-Good evening-Good night" to the children. Let them know the differences. Then, teach these greetings one by one. Do it by chorus first, then have two students role-play it till all the children are familiar with the above greetings.

1-1 LET'S PRACTICE

Look and say.

8:00

John: Good morning, Mary.
Mary: Good morning, John.

9:00

3:00

8:00

11:00

Note: Let children point to the pictures and say them aloud. You can divide the whole class into two groups-girls as Mary and boys as John. After a group drill, have one boy and one girl practice.

two

1-2 SING A SONG

Good Morning to You

Note: Remind the children that this melody is similar to the song: "Happy Birth-day to You". You can change the lyrics to other greetings. Students can sing back to you in chorus or individually. Let them sing to one another as well.

■**本單元目標：**一天生活的開始，必須交換「問候」。學習英語會話的第一步，也必須練習Good morning,Good afternoon,Good evening,Good night等問候語，直到説得流利為止。

■**在家學習的方法：**首先，請媽媽幫助小朋友作練習。問候語之後通常要加上對方的名字。小朋友向媽媽問候時，要加上Mommy，而媽媽向小朋友問候時，則加上小朋友的名字，例如：

• 小朋友：Good morning, Mommy.
• 媽媽：Good morning, John.

依序作Good afternoon,Good evening,Good night 等練習。在平時，更應隨時作這些問候練習，以養成習慣。

2. WHAT'S YOUR NAME ?

Note: Point to yourself, say: "My name is _____." Repeat several times. Let them then repeat: "My name is _____." After reciting in chorus point to individual students and say: My name is _____. What's your name?" Use "Chain-conversations" to let the students practice one by one. Then introduce "His name is_____." Directly after a boy's saying"My name is _____."Work with more boys; have the class repeat"His name is _____"in chorus each time. Practice"Her name is_____"in the same way. Finally, point to a student and ask: What's his/her name? to let them answer. Lastly have some children role-play the above dialogue.

2-1 LET'S PRACTICE
Questions and answers.

What's his name ?
His name is Peter.

What's her name ?
Her name is Mary.

Note: Your can ask them "What's his/her name?" as you point to the person on this page. Let them point to the person on the page and say the answer aloud.

2-2 SING A SONG

BINGO

There was a far—mer had a dog. And BIN-GO was his name. Oh!

B — I — N-G — O, B — I — N-G — O,

B — I — N — G — O. And BIN-GO was his name. Oh!

Note: You can ask them "What's his/her name?" as you point to the person "O". The second time, clap twice instead of saying "G-O", and the student who makes a mistake will be out of the game. After the fifth clapping, look who is the winner.

■**本單元目標：**學習自我介紹及詢問對方名字的問答
1. What's your name?　　3. His name is～.
2. My name is～.　　　　4. Her name is～.

■**在家學習的方法：**請反覆發問What's your name?直到孩子能够流利回答My name is～.為止。這時，請不要忘記也自我介紹My name is～.
倘若爸爸也來參加，則能做下列快樂的練習。

- 媽：My name is～. What's your name?
- 子：My name is～. What's his name?
- 媽：His name is～.
- 爸：My name is～. What's her name?
- 子：Her name is～.

依照上列循環，可以改變順序，並作速答比賽。

3. ALPHABET (1)

	A APPLE	**B** BOY
C CAT	**D** DOG	**E** EGG
F FISH	**G** GIRL	**H** HAT
I ICE CREAM	**J** JAR	**K** KING
L LION	**M** MAN	**N** NEWSPAPER

O ORANGE	P PENCIL	Q QUEEN
R RABBIT	S SHIP	T TIGER
U UMBRELLA	V VIOLIN	W WOMAN
X X-RAY	Y YOLK	Z ZEBRA

Note: For the alphabet, point to the pictures and repeat the word aloud. Write the word on the board and have the students spell it out.

3-1 LET'S PRACTICE

Look and say.

3-2 SING A SONG

THE ALPHABET

Note: First of all, the teacher should guide the students in reading the alphabet in four parts/ABCDEFG/,/HIJKLMNOP/,/QRSTUV/,/W and XYZ/. After practicing three times, sing it wholly to the student. Then, lead the students to sing it part by part. Finally, let them sing the whole song.

3-3 EXERCISE

Dot to dot.

Start with the letter A.
Draw a line to join up the dots in order from A to Z.

■本單元目標：認識各英文大寫字母，每個字母輔以圖片練習，加強印象，直到小朋友對
　字母與實物均能作直接反應為止。
■在家學習的方法：首先，媽媽以課本上的圖片讓小朋友識別各個字母，連同實物，一
　併說出名稱，反覆練習至熟練為止，練習時可不按順序。

4. ALPHABET (2)

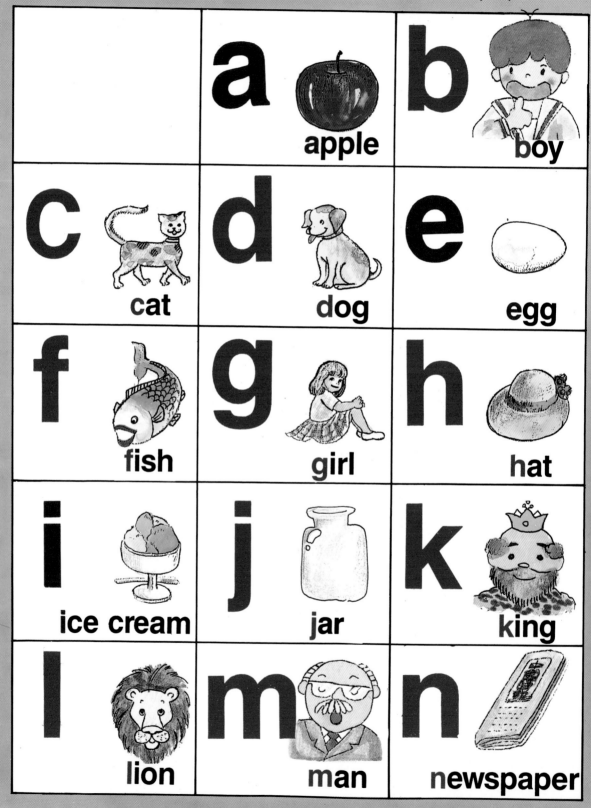

	a apple	b boy
c cat	d dog	e egg
f fish	g girl	h hat
i ice cream	j jar	k king
l lion	m man	n newspaper

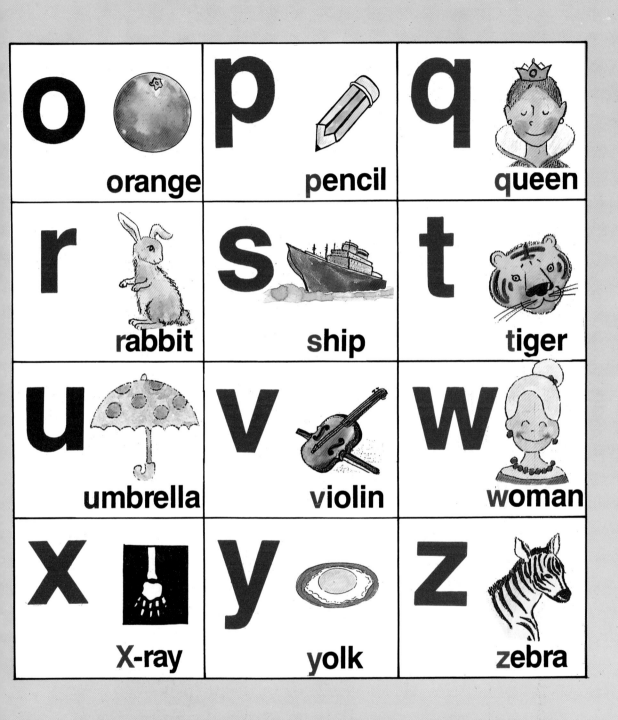

o orange	p pencil	q queen
rabbit	ship	t tiger
umbrella	violin	woman
X-ray	yolk	zebra

Note: For this unit, you can have students review the pictures by saying them aloud. And remind them of capital letters.

4-1 LET'S PRACTICE

Fill in the small letters.

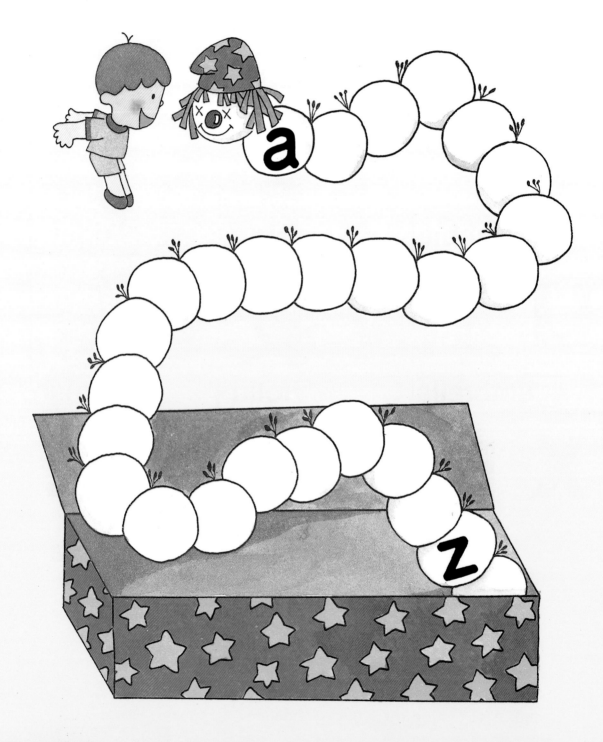

4-2 PLAY A GAME

BINGO

Note: First of all, fill the blanks with twenty five small letters from a to y (the order depends on the student). Draw circles around each letter as you read the letters. When someone completes three lines, he can raise his or her hand and say "Bingo!".(Another way is to have them choose any 25 of the 26 letters).

4-3 EXERCISE

1. Draw a circle.

An apple ?	**A cat ?**	**A fish ?**
Yes　　No	Yes　　No	Yes　　No
A king ?	**A tiger ?**	**An egg ?**
Yes　　No	Yes　　No	Yes　　No

2. Fill the blanks.

1. b c □
2. e □ g
3. □ i j
4. r s □
5. w x □

3. Look and join.

D T Q G B H N

g b h d t q n

■**本單元目標：**認識英文小寫字母，並複習前次單元所列舉之實物。

■**在家學習的方法：**先複習大寫字母，再以大寫字母來練習其相對之小寫字母。並且，
要連同實物一起練習，以加深印象。

5. NUMBERS (1)

Note: First of all, teach them how to say these numbers. Write the numbers one at a time on the board, saying the number as you do so. Ask individual student to come to the board and write the number when you say it. Let the students write down any number they wish from 1 to 10 on a piece of paper, calling out numbers at random: "Number two, stand up!" (All the students who have chosen that number will stand and hold up the number.)

1 one	2 two
3 three	4 four
5 five	6 six
7 seven	8 eight
9 nine	10 ten

Note: Write the words for the numbers one at a time on the board, also saying the number as you do so. Point to each word on the board so students' attention will be focused on the word. Then put the words for the numbers at random. Now point to the words and ask individual students to tell you which number to write next to each. Continue until you feel sure that students are really reading and not just guessing.

5-1 LET'S PRACTICE

Learn this rhyme.

Numbers: Learn this rhyme.

① Number one.
Look at the sun.

② Number two.
This is my shoe.

③ Number three.
It's a tree.

④ Number four.
Open the door.

⑤ Number five.
It's alive!

⑥ Number six.
Pick up the sticks.

⑦ Number seven.
Draw a seven.

⑧ Number eight.
Close the gate.

⑨ Number nine.
Draw a line.

⑩ Number ten.
Stop my hen!

GAME

5-2 SING A SONG

Ten Little Indians

One lit-tle, two lit-tle, three lit-tle In-dians,
Ten lit-tle, nine lit-tle, eight lit-tle In-dians,

four — lit-tle, five lit-tle, six lit-tle In-dians,
sev-en lit-tle, six lit-tle, five lit-tle In-dians,

sev-en lit-tle, eight lit-tle, nine lit-tle In-dians,
four — lit-tle, three lit-tle, two lit-tle In-dians,

ten lit-tle In-dian boys(girls).
one lit-tle In-dian boy (girl).

Note: Teach each part of the song and repeat until each student can sing the song from memory. Have students use their fingers to show the numbers while they are singing.

5-3 EXERCISE

Look and write.

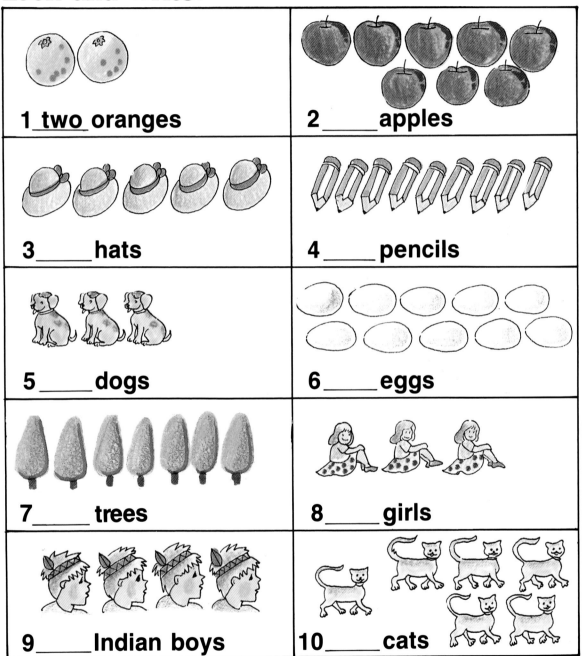

1 _two_ oranges

2 _____ apples

3 _____ hats

4 _____ pencils

5 _____ dogs

6 _____ eggs

7 _____ trees

8 _____ girls

9 _____ Indian boys

10 _____ cats

■本單元目標：學習英語 1 到 10 的講法及各數目字的寫法。

■在家學習的方法：媽媽先唸給小朋友聽，等小朋友熟悉了一到十的說法後，可用手指頭比出一個數目，讓小朋友說英語的講法，或由媽媽說出數字，而小朋友用手指頭比，使他完全熟悉為止。同時，利用課本上的圖案，讓小朋友先讀出數字，再認清一到十的寫法。詩歌部分，可用拍手來掌握節拍，增加趣味。

6. NUMBERS (2)

11 eleven 10

12 twelve 10

13 thirteen 10

14 fourteen 10

15 fifteen 10

16 sixteen 10

17 seventeen 10

18 eighteen 10

19 nineteen 10

20 twenty 10

Note: Warm up by counting from 1 to 10. Then, let the students count numbers 11 to 20 aloud after you. Draw groups of things on the board and have the students count the number of things on the board.

21 twenty-one
22 twenty-two
23 twenty-three
24 twenty-four
25 twenty-five
26 twenty-six
27 twenty-seven
28 twenty-eight
29 twenty-nine

30 thirty
40 forty
50 fifty
60 sixty
70 seventy
80 eighty
90 ninety
100 one hundred

one hundred

three six two — o /o/ five three seven

seven eighty-eight — nineteen twenty-nine

ninety-seven

Note: Teach numbers twenty-one to one hundred. For practicing numbers, you will find dots and crosses useful since these can quickly be placed on the board. For higher numbers, examples can be written on the board e.g. 78, 84. Then, you can use telephone and car numbers or some other numbers found on objects in the classroom to familiarize them with numbers.

6-1 LET'S PRACTICE

Say the numbers.

I am one hundred!

I am ninety.

I am eighty.

I am seventy.

I am sixty.

I am fifty.

I am forty.

I am thirty.

I am twenty.

I am ten.

6-2 PLAY A GAME
Join, point and say.

6-3 EXERCISE

A. Say.

What's the telephone number ?

B. Write.

1. How much is this cat ? 2. How much is this dog ? 3. How much is this rabbit ?

It is＿＿＿ dollars.　It is＿＿＿ dollars.　It is＿＿＿ dollars.

■本單元目標：認識數目字11～100的讀法及寫法。同時，讓小朋友學習電話號碼、車號日常用物之讀法。

■在家學習的方法：媽媽先幫助小朋友複習１～10的説法。接著練習11～20, 21～100,反覆練習至熟練爲止。另外，可利用家中的電話、車號來熟悉數字的説法。

7. WHAT TIME IS IT ?

What time is it ?

It is six forty.

What time is it ?

It is seven o'clock.

What time is it ?

It's seven forty-five.

What time is it ?   **It's four fifteen.**

What time is it ?   **It's seven twenty.**

What time is it ?   **It's nine thirty.**

Note: For teaching time, use a model clock if available. If not, use simple drawings on the blackboard. Let them be familiar with the question: "What time is it?" Teach them also how to tell time at this stage.

7-1 LET'S PRACTICE

Look at the clock and write the time.

7-2 SING A SONG

HICKORY, DICKORY, DOCK

7-③ EXERCISE

A. Look and write the time.

1. _____
2. _____
3. _____

B. Look and draw the hands.

It's six o'clock.

It's four thirty.

It's ten thirty.

It's eight ten.

It's nine forty.

It's seven twenty.

■ **本單元目標**：使小朋友熟悉各時間的各種說法。
■ **在家學習的方法**：除了書本上的說寫練習之外，請媽媽隨時問小朋友 `What time is it？' 或者做某些行為（如吃晚餐、上學……等等）的時間，使小朋友熟練自如。

8. WHAT IS THIS ?

This is a robot.

This is a bag.

This is a book.

This is a cup.

This is a ruler.

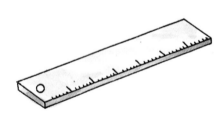

This is a duck.

This is a hen.

This is a pen.

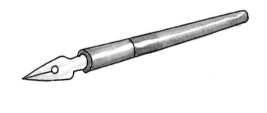

Note: First teach "This is _____." using objects that they have already learned. Be sure that the object is touched or held as the sentences are spoken. If blackboard drawings are used, you should be standing near the drawings as you ask or speak. The students must come to the board when they speak. Do not let students remain in their seats, point at the board and say, "This is _____."

WHAT IS THAT ?

That is a kite.

That is a bird.

That is an elephant.

That is an eraser.

That is a chair.

That is a blackboard.

That is a house.

That is a desk.

Note: It is very important to use "That is" when the student speaks about something that is some distance away.

8-1 LET'S PRACTICE
What is this ?

Fill in the blanks.

8-2 PLAY A GAME

Hit the Bat

	4	7
2		8
3		9

Note: First of all, draw a square such as the one on above the board and divide the whole class into two groups. Tell them to choose one number as their group's danger number. You alone should know what the two numbers are. Then, choose one child from each group to go in front to represent group. Use the picture card or drawings on the book to ask: "What is this?" The two children have to raise their hands and the one who raises their hand first gets to answer the question. If he/she is right, the other one must choose one number. If he/she is wrong, the other group gets to answer. If the answer is right, the first group has to choose two numbers. Go on the game until one of them hits the danger number.

8-3 EXERCISE

A. Questions and answers.

1. What is this?	2. What ___ ___ ?	3. ___ ___ ___ ?

This is a ___.	This is ___ ___ .	___ ___ ___ .

B. Draw and write.

1. Draw a pencil.	2. Draw a fish.	3. Draw ice cream.
This is ___ ___.	This ___ ___ ___ .	___ ___ ___ ___ .

■本單元目標：學習指著自己附近的東西説「這是～」以及較遠的東西説「那是～」的説法。

　1.What is this?　This is～.
　2.What is that?　That is～.

■在家學習的方法：選擇小朋友認識的實物，由媽媽發問〝What is this(that)?〞而由小朋友回答：〝This(That)is～〞使小朋友熟悉物體在遠、近距離時所應採用的句型。

9. IS THIS A BALL ?

Note: Use the question "Is this _____ ?" for vocabulary review using objects, pictures or blackboard drawings. Then teach students to answer the questions, repeating after the teacher. After this, hold up or point to an object or picture and name it. The class then, in chorus or individually, asks and the teacher answers. The same conversation can take place between students in the class. Students can call each other by name, too.

IS THAT A TELEPHONE ?

Is that a telephone ?
Yes, it is.
It is a telephone.

Is that a tree ?
No, it is not.
It is not a tree.
It is a flower.

Is that a bird ?
No, it is not.
It is not a bird.
It is a bee.

Is that a cake ?
Yes, it is.
It is a cake.

Note: Be sure that when you and your students use "that", the object of picture is some distance away. As usual, do not "read" the pictures in these pages until all the students can ask and answer the sentences correctly.

9-1 LET'S PRACTICE

Look and answer.

Is this a bicycle ?

Is this an eraser ?

Is this a table ?

Is this a duck ?

Is this a fish ?

Is this a cake ?

Is this a tiger ?

Is this a piano ?

9-2 PLAY A GAME

Note: There are many variations in these "Question and Answer" games. For example, the teacher may think of an object, or a student may think of an object and draw it on the board. At first, do not complete the drawing, members of the class can then ask "Is that a ball?" "Is that a ruler?" etc, until someone guesses the right anwer. This may be played in teams.

9-3 EXERCISE

Questions and answers.

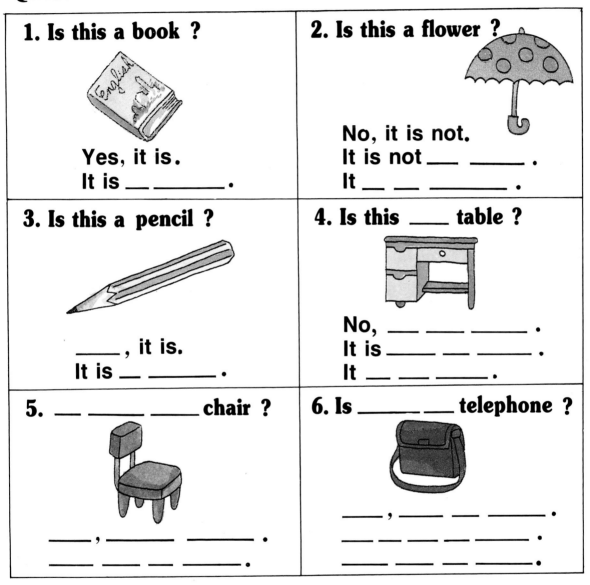

1. Is this a book ?

Yes, it is .
It is __ _____ .

2. Is this a flower ?

No, it is not.
It is not __ _____ .
It __ __ _____ .

3. Is this a pencil ?

_____ , it is.
It is __ _____ .

4. Is this ____ table ?

No, _____ _____ .
It is _____ _____ .
It __ __ _____ .

5. __ _____ _____ chair ?

_____ , _____ _____ .
__ __ _____ _____ .

6. Is _____ __ telephone ?

_____ , _____ _____ .
__ __ _____ _____ .

■本單元目標：學習使用`Is that~?″和`Is this~?″的問句及`Yes″或`No.″的回答方式，本單元的主要句型為：
1.Is that (this)~?
2.Yes, it is. It is~.
3.No, it is not. It is not~. It is~.

■在家學習的方法：媽媽在幫助小朋友學習時，可與第八單元學過的句型交互使用，使小朋友熟習二種問句的回答方式。同時，藉以幫助小朋友複習曾經學過的單字與認識新的名詞。

10. PARTS OF MY BODY (1)

My name is A-Da.

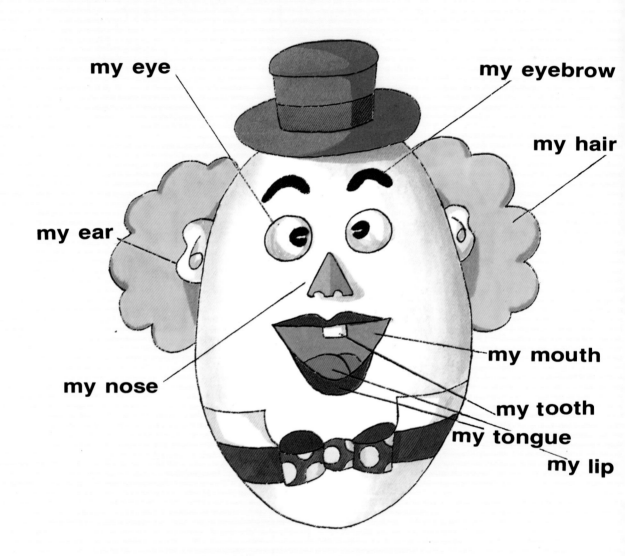

my eye

my eyebrow

my hair

my ear

my nose

my mouth

my tooth

my tongue

my lip

This is my face.

Note: Teach "This is my hair", "This is my ear" etc. one at a time. Touch each part of your body as you say the words. Let the children do the same as they repeat after you. Then, the teacher should simply point to a part of her body and the students should say the appropriate sentence while doing the same.

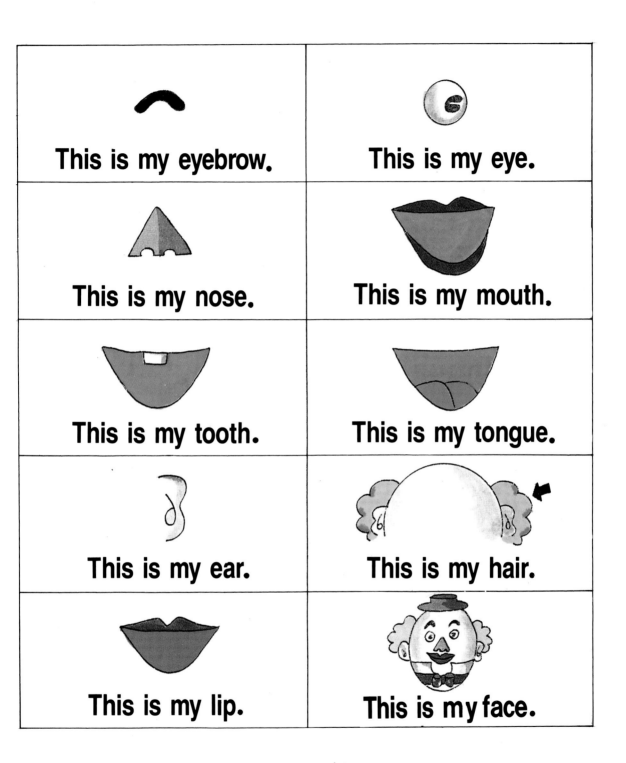

This is my eyebrow.

This is my eye.

This is my nose.

This is my mouth.

This is my tooth.

This is my tongue.

This is my ear.

This is my hair.

This is my lip.

This is my face.

Note: After practicing these, you play the game "Action Chain". The first student touches a part of his body and says: "This is my _____ ." Continue this around the class.

10-1 LET'S PRACTICE

Please draw.

Draw hair.	Draw a nose.	Draw a mouth.
Draw an eye.	Draw a tooth.	Draw an ear.
Draw a lip.	Draw a tongue.	Draw an eyebrow.

10-2 SING A SONG

Head,Shoulders, knees and toes

Note: As they sing this song, they should touch their heads, shoulders, etc. This song can be sung faster and faster, until everyone is really out of breath and really "awake" from all the stretching and bending.

10-③ EXERCISE

A. Look at the picture and circle the correct word.

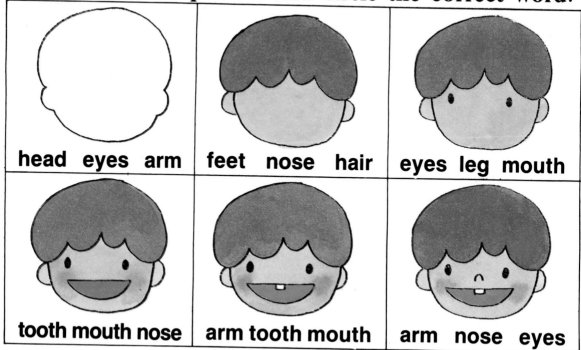

head eyes arm	feet nose hair	eyes leg mouth
tooth mouth nose	arm tooth mouth	arm nose eyes

B. Draw and write.

Please draw your face.

■**本單元目標**：認識臉上各部位的説法及寫法。
■**在家學習的方法**：媽媽可用手，指著孩子臉上的某一部位，問小朋友〝What is this?〞而由小朋友回答〝This is my nose／mouth／eye／ear……etc.〞直到小朋友完全熟悉臉上五官的名稱為止。

11. PARTS OF MY BODY (11)

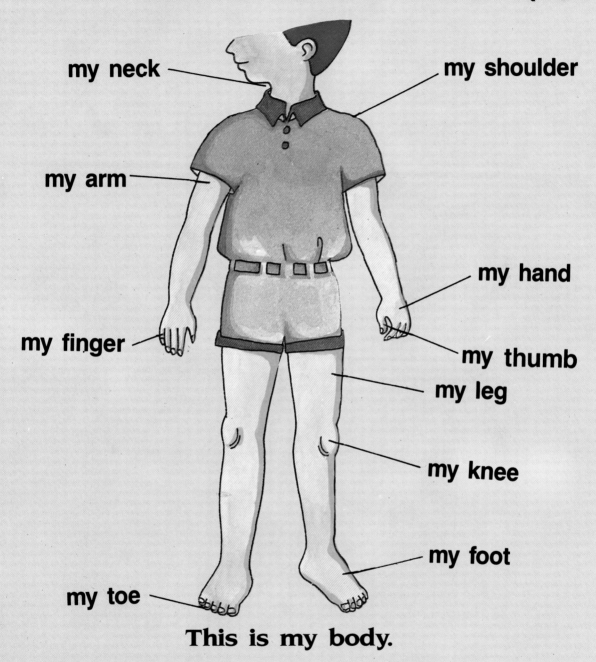

my neck

my shoulder

my arm

my hand

my finger

my thumb

my leg

my knee

my foot

my toe

This is my body.

Note: Follow the last unit's procedures. Both teacher and students should touch the part of their body they are speaking about. Then, the teacher should simply point to the part of the body and let the students say the appropriate sentence while doing the same. Finally, practice in a chain. Let the first student touch a part of his body and say "This is my_____." Then he points to a different part of the next child's body who then has to say "This is my_____." Continue this around the class.

 **1. This is my neck.**	 **2. This is my shoulder.**
 **3. This is my arm.**	 **4. This is my hand.**
5. This is my thumb.	**6. This is my finger.**
7. This is my leg.	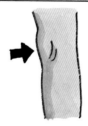 **8. This is my knee.**
 **9. This is my foot.**	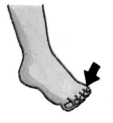 **10. This is my toe.**

11-1 LET'S PRACTICE

Point and say.

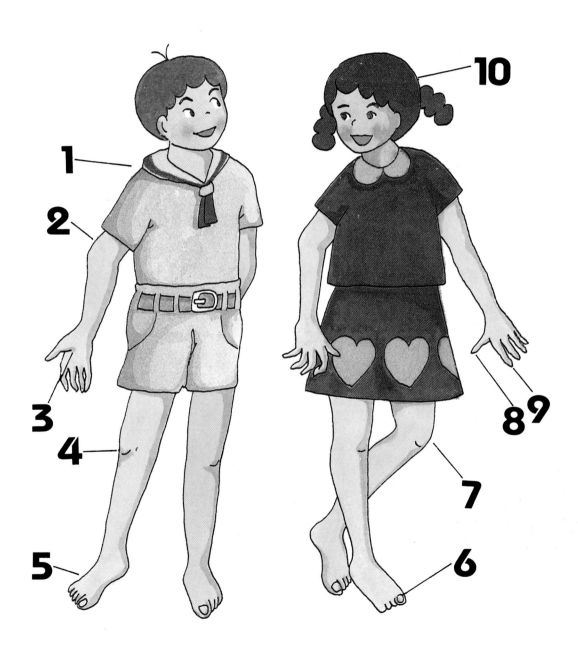

11-2 PLAY A GAME
three riddles
What am I ?

1. I have one long hand.
   I have one short hand.
   I don't have ears.
   I am a_____ .

2. I have one big mouth.
   I have one arm.
   I don't have feet.
   I am a ____ .

3. I have four thick legs.
   I have one long nose.
   I don't have fingers.
   I am an_____ .

Note: First of all, read these sentences and explain simply the unfamiliar objects.
Let the students guess what the correct answer is. Then, let them read
the above sentences.

11-③ EXERCISE

A. Complete the sentences.

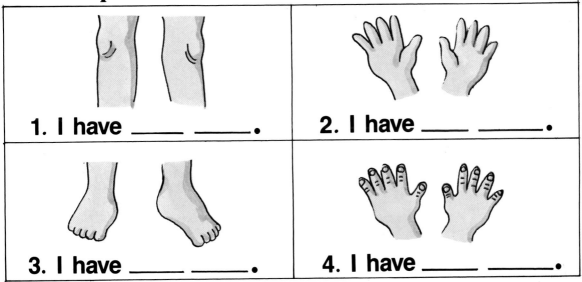

1. I have ＿＿＿ ＿＿＿ .

2. I have ＿＿＿ ＿＿＿ .

3. I have ＿＿＿ ＿＿＿ .

4. I have ＿＿＿ ＿＿＿ .

B. Join lines.

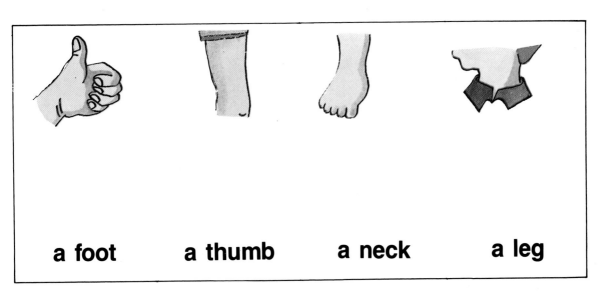

a foot　　a thumb　　a neck　　a leg

■本單元目標：學習身體各部位的說法。

■在家學習的方媽媽先指著自己的脖子說：〝This is my neck.〞孩子也跟著指自己的脖子，並說〝This is my neck.〞依此方法，完成各部位的練習。然後媽媽用手指著小朋友身體之部位，小朋友則依著所指而說〝This is my～.〞反覆練習至熟悉為止。

12. MY FAMILY

My name is Mary.
This is my family.

This is my mother.

This is my father.

This is my brother.

This is my sister.

Note: Teach the new words: father, mother, brother and sister using blackboard drawings. Explain in the student's own language or through pictures in the book.

Point and say.

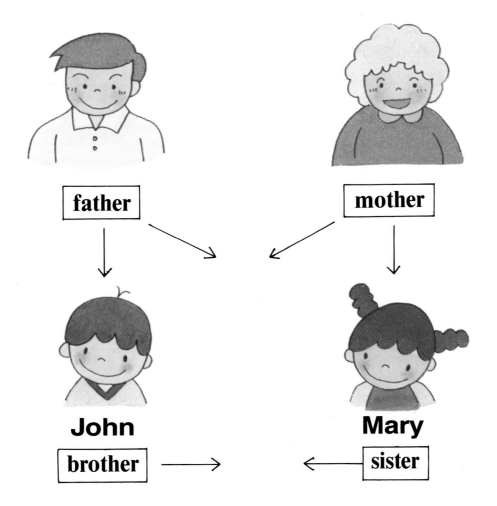

My name is John.

This is my father.

This is my mother.

This is my sister.

My name is Mary.

This is my father.

This is my mother.

This is my brother.

Note: After the children familiarize themselves with these sentence patterns, role-play them. Let one boy be John and one girl be Mary. Point to the above pictures or draw their family members on the board and let them say them aloud.

12-1 LET'S PRACTICE

Fill in the blanks.

Point and say.

This is my _____.

My name is John.

12-2 SING A SONG

Where is father ?

Where is fa-ther ? Where is fa-ther? Here I am!
(mo-ther)   (mo-ther)
(bro-ther)   (bro-ther)
(sis-ter)   (sis-ter)

Here I am!   How are you this morn-ing?

Ver-y well I thank you. Run a-way,   run a-way!

Note: First, remind the students that the melody of this song is like the Chinese song "Two Tigers".

12-③ EXERCISE

Paste, write and say.

Paste your photo here.

My name is ____.

Paste your father's photo here.

Paste your mother's photo here.

This is my ____.

This is ___ ____.

Paste your brother's photo here.

Paste your sister's photo here.

This __ ___ ____.

____ ___ ____ ____.

■**本單元目標：**學習簡單介紹自己家人的方法
 1.My name is～.
 2.This is my～.

■**在家學習的方法：**當小朋友學會了father,mother,brother,sister,等稱謂後，取出一張紙，讓小朋友將每位家人作簡單的素描，然後由媽媽一一指著圖上人物，反覆練習 ˋThis is my～.″ 如果家人都在時，可以指定其中一位爲客人，由小朋友把每一位家人介紹給這位客人，被介紹者，請以「點頭」或各種姿勢回答。

13. I AM... YOU ARE...

This is John.   This is Mary.

I am John.   **I am Mary.**
I am a boy.   **I am a girl.**

Note: Begin by saying "I am Miss _____ , Mr. _____ " etc. Now, review "I am"
with names and point to individual students, say "I am Miss _____", and
get each student to say "I am _____ ." Then teach "I am a boy" and "I
am a girl", follow the same procedure as above, Go around the class and
let each student say one of the two sentences.

I am Mark. **I am Susan.**

You are Susan. **You are Mark.**

I am a boy.
You are a girl.

I am a girl.
You are a boy.

Note: When giving the model, "you are", have a child out in the front and point to the child when saying "You are _____". Repeat the expression with the children pointing to the same child. On their own, tell a student to stand up and the rest of the students to point and speak to him/her. Let the students practice in pairs and have them converse in a chain.

13-1 LET'S PRACTICE

Do and say.

Note: Two at a time, one student is blindfolded. The student who cannot see tries to guess who is the one behind him or her. Let this go on around the class.

13-2 PLAY A GAME
Do a Role-play

Note: Before the class, prepare two crowns for this role-play. Give some explanations and then ask and answer questions yourself first. And then let the students do it among themselves.

13-3 EXERCISE

Write and say.

John

Mary

I am ____ .
I am __ ____ .

I am ____ .
__ __ ____ .

You are ____ .
__ __ __ ____ .

You __ ____ .
__ __ __ ____ .

Draw yourself here.

____ ____ . (What is your name?)

(Are you a boy or
a girl?)
__ __ __ __ ____ .

■本單元目標：學習自我介紹及簡單敍述對方的方法
1.I am~. I am a~.   2.You are~. You are a~.
■在家學習的方法：請反覆發問 What is your name?
Are you a boy or a girl?直到孩子能够流利回答 I am~. I am a~.爲止。請不要忘記先自我介紹
I am? I am a~.再以手勢來問 What is my name? Am I a boy or a girl?直到孩子能很快地説出 You
are~. You are a~.

14. HE IS... SHE IS...

1.

> **He is a boy.**
> **He is Mark.**

2.

> **She is a girl.**
> **She is Susan.**

3.

> **He is a man.**
> **He is Mr. Lee.**

4.

> **She is a woman.**
> **She is Mrs. Ling.**

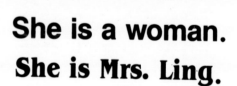 

Note: First teach "He is a boy" and "She is a girl". Bring some boys and girls to the front. Point to one of them as you read the sentences. Follow the usual procedure, but make sure that the students point to a boy or a girl as they speak. Next teach "He is Mark", "She is Susan". Repeat until each student can point to another student and say the pair of sentences: "He is a boy" and "He is Mark". Use pictures in the book to teach the remaining pairs of sentences.

1. She is a teacher.

2. He is a policeman.

3. He is a doctor.

4. She is a nurse.

5. He is a farmer.

6. He is a mailman.

Note: Read the occupations listed above while the students look at the pictures. Then practice more by using simple drawings on the board. Make these as simple as possible. Say the occupations several times as you do the drawings. When pictures of all the occupations have been drawn, use the pictures as cues. As you point, the class says "He/She is a doctor /a teacher," etc.

14-1 LET'S PRACTICE

Draw, write and read.

John

Mary

Mr. Lee

Mrs. Ling

Mark

1.

He is ___ ____.
He is ____.

2.

She is ___ ____.
She is ____.

3.

_____.
_____.

4.

_____.
_____.

5.

_____.
_____.

14-2 PLAY A GAME

Note: One child can be blindfolded or can stand in a corner with his/her back
to the class. The teacher points to a student who says something such as
"This is a book". (This is an opportunity for a vocabulary review.)The
student who cannot see, tries to guess who has spoken and says: "He is a boy,
he is John", etc. When he guesses correctly, someone else takes his place.

14-3 EXERCISE

Circle and read.

1.

He
She is a   boy.
            girl.

2.

He
She is a   man.
            woman.

3.

He
She is a   doctor.
            nurse.

4.

He
She is a   mailman.
            farmer.

5.

He
She is a   nurse.
            teacher.

■ **本單元目標：**學習介紹第三者的方法及六種職業的說法。

　1.He is～.

　2.She is～.

■ **在家學習的方法：**利用課本上的圖畫讓孩子練習 He is～.及She is～.不依順序、反覆練習至孩子能很快地說出兩句 He/She is a～. He/She is～.職業部分，也依同樣方法使其熟練 He 和She的用法。

R-1 REVIEW
PICTURE PRACTICE (point and say)

This is a classroom.

R-2
PICTURE PRACTICE (point and say)

This is a room.

R-3
LOOK AND WRITE

1. ___a cat___

2. _____

3. _____

4. _____

5. _____

6. _____

7. _____

8. _____

9. _____

10. _____

11. _____

12. _____

13. _____

14. _____

15. _____

16. _____

17. _____

18. _____

R-4
A CROSSWORD PUZZLE

R-5
PICTURE DICTIONARY

1. an apple	2. an arm	3. a bag	4. a ball
5. a bee	6. a bicycle	7. a bird	8. a blackboard
9. a book	10. a car	11. a cat	12. a chair
13. a cup	14. a desk	15. a doctor	16. a door
17. a duck	18. an ear	19. an egg	20. an elephant

21. an eraser	22. an eye	23. an eyebrow	24. a face
25. a farmer	26. a finger	27. a fish	28. a flower
29. a foot	30. a gate	31. a girl	32. hair
33. a hand	34. a hat	35. a hen	36. a house
37. ice cream	38. a jar	39. a king	40. a kite

41. a knee	42. a leg	43. a lion	44. a lip
45. a mailman	46. a man	47. a mouth	48. a neck
49. a newspaper	50. a nose	51. a nurse	52. an orange
53. a pen	54. a pencil	55. a piano	56. a policeman
57. a queen	58. a rabbit	59. a robot	60. a ruler

61. a ship	62. a shoe	63. a shoulder	64. a stick
65. the sun	66. a table	67. a teacher	68. a tooth
69. a telephone	70. a thumb	71. a tiger	72. a toe
73. a tongue	74. a tree	75. an umbrella	76. a violin
77. a woman	78. an X-ray	79. a yolk	80. a zebra

第 一 册 學 習 內 容 一 覽 表

單元	內 容	練 習	活 動	習 作
1	問 候 語	Look and say: Good morning, afternoon, evening, night.	歌曲：Good morning to you	本單元注重口說練習
2	你的名字叫什麼？	練習 Questions and answers: What is his/her name? His/Her name is ～.	歌曲：BINGO	本單元注重口說練習
3	大 寫 字 母	Look and say: 從物體中找出大寫字母	歌曲：The alphabet song	Dot to dot: A～Z.
4	小 寫 字 母	Fill in the small letters: 寫 a～z	遊戲：Bingo（賓果）	Draw, write and join.
5	數字：一～十	Learn this rhyme.（數字）	歌曲：Ten Little Indians	Look and write.
6	數字：十一～一百	Say the numbers: 練習 11…100 的說法	遊戲：Join, point, say.	Read and write.
7	現在是幾點幾分？	Look and write: What time is it?	歌曲：Hickory, dickory, dock.	Look, write and draw.
8	這是什麼？那是什麼？	Fill in the blanks: What is this? This is a ～.（東西）	遊戲：Hit the bat.（強棒出擊）	Draw and write.
9	這是一個球嗎？那是一個電話嗎？	Look and answer: Is this a ～? Yes、No 的答法	遊戲：A guessing game.	Questions and answers.
10	我 的 臉	Please draw: 依指示畫下臉上的某一部分	歌曲：Head, shoulders, knees and toes.	Circle and write.
11	我 的 身 體	Point and say: 指著圖中人物說：This is his/her ～.（身體部位）	遊戲：Three riddles.	Write and join.
12	我 的 家 人	Write, point and say: This is my ～.（家人）	歌曲：Where is father?	Paste, write and say.
13	我是個男孩 你是個女孩	Do and say: 練習 I am ～. You are ～.	遊戲：Do a role-play.	Write and say.
14	他是個男人 她是個女人	Draw, write and read: 練習 He is ～. She is ～.	遊戲：A guessing game.	Circle and read.
複習	看圖練習 看圖練習 看圖練習 縱橫字謎 生字總復習	Point and say. Point and say. Look and write. A crossword puzzle. Picture dictionary.		

獲 國立教育資料館審核通過！

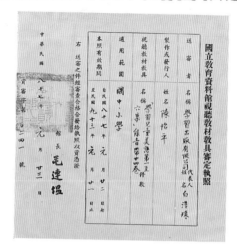

學習兒童美語讀本①
LEARNING
English Readers for Children

書＋MP3 一片售價：280 元

編　　著／陳 怡 平
發 行 所／學習出版有限公司　　☎ (02) 2704-5525
郵 撥 帳 號／05127272 學習出版社帳戶
登 記 證／局版台業 2179 號
印 刷 所／裕強彩色印刷有限公司
台 北 門 市／台北市許昌街 17 號 6F　　☎ (02) 2331-4060
台灣總經銷／紅螞蟻圖書有限公司　　☎ (02) 2795-3656
本公司網址／www.learnbook.com.tw
電 子 郵 件／learnbook@learnbook.com.tw

2022 年 3 月 1 日新修訂

ISBN 978-957-519-970-8